Rapunzel's Heroes

By Ellie O'Ryan

Illustrated by The Disney Storybook Artists

Disney PRESS

New York

*R*apunzel had one wish for her birthday: to see the beautiful lights that floated above the kingdom every year for one night only. And today, it seemed like her wish was going to come true! A young man named Flynn Rider had agreed to take her to see them.

But there was just one problem. Flynn was in a lot of trouble . . . and a palace horse named Maximus was determined to bring him to justice!

Rapunzel knew that she'd never see
the sparkling lights if Maximus got Flynn
in trouble. "Easy, boy, easy," she said
softly. "You're a good boy, aren't you?"
Rapunzel's chameleon friend Pascal
looked at Maximus and smiled.

"Look, today is kind of the biggest day of my life," Rapunzel explained. "And the thing is, I need you *not* to get Flynn arrested. Just for twenty-four hours, and then you can chase each other to your heart's content. Okay? And it's kind of my birthday . . . just so you know." Rapunzel reached out and gave Maximus a hug.

The horse just snorted. As far as he was concerned, Flynn Rider was a thief who belonged in jail! But even Maximus couldn't resist Rapunzel's kindness. He stuck out his hoof to shake with Flynn.

However, the truce ended when Flynn decided to jump onto Maximus's back. The horse bucked, tossing Flynn right into a giant puddle!

Flynn shook himself off. He stood up and hopped onto the horse's back again. He was furious!

Maximus tossed Flynn off his back for the second time. Rapunzel was worried. If Flynn and Maximus kept fighting, she'd never get to the kingdom and see the lights! Then she had an idea: maybe she could teach them how to be friends.

First, Rapunzel showed Flynn how to stroke Maximus's forehead and scratch behind his ears. Then she asked the horse to give Flynn another chance.

Flynn started scratching Maximus's head. Neither he nor the horse looked happy, but at least no one landed in a puddle!

Now that everyone was getting along, the group headed to the kingdom. Maximus had the perfect opportunity to get Flynn in trouble. But then he remembered what Rapunzel had said. The horse decided to help Flynn sneak past the guards.

For Rapunzel, spending her birthday in the kingdom was full of wonderful surprises and adventures! After her beautiful long hair was tied back with ribbons and pretty flowers, Rapunzel and Flynn danced through the town square!

A little while later, Maximus's ears perked up when he heard a strange cry. The horse galloped off, with Flynn following right behind him. When they found a scared kitten stuck in a tree, Flynn and Maximus worked together to rescue it.

As the golden sun started to set, Flynn and Rapunzel climbed into a small boat to watch the lights over the water. Flynn tossed Maximus an apple and smiled. Rapunzel grinned as the first lights drifted through the starry sky. Thanks to her friends, this was the best birthday she could have imagined!